KT-424-732

This Winnie-the-Pooh
book belongs to

....

EGMONT

We bring stories to life

First Published in Great Britain 2018 by Egmont UK Limited
The Yellow Building, 1 Nicholas Road, London W11 4AN

Written by Jane Riordan
Designed by Pritty Ramjee
Illustrated by Eleanor Taylor and Mikki Butterley
Copyright © 2018 Disney Enterprises, Inc.
Based on the "Winnie the Pooh" works
by A.A.Milne and E.H.Shepard

ISBN 978 1 4052 9109 5
68697/002
Printed in Italy

Winnie-the-Pooh

The Long
Winter's Sleep

EGMONT

A cold wind blew through the Hundred Acre Wood. It tugged at the last few leaves as they clung to the branches. The leaves had held on for so long, but this wind was different, it was a wintery north wind and it soon won the battle and the leaves were whisked away.

It was in this **blustery** weather that little Piglet hurried through the Forest.

Piglet was a Very Small Animal and a gust of wind was quite enough to knock him right over. He was much happier when his feet were at the bottom and his ears were at the top. He didn't much want to be any other way round which was why he was in such a rush to get out of the wind that day.

When Piglet finally reached his house, he gathered writing materials and scratched out the following message:

COLD. IN BED.
BAK IN SRPING. Piglit

He pinned the note to his door and, as if the wind had read his message, a sudden flurry blew the little Piglet into his house, **banging** the door shut behind him.

In another part of the Forest, Pooh was also feeling a little **shivery**.

He decided to play at hunting Heffalumps under the covers of his bed. But it was so warm and snug there, and the Hefflalumps weren't the **ferocious** kind, just the dozy kind, and so it wasn't long before Pooh was in a deep sleep.

The others had sensed the change in the weather, as well.

Rabbit in his perfectly-tidy burrow …

Tigger, Kanga and Roo in their little home ...

And even Eeyore, the old, grey donkey,
in his house of sticks ...

... were all settling down for a long
winter's sleep.

As the sun set behind the Six Pine Trees,
a deep silence fell over the Forest.

But somebody

or something

wasn't asleep...

Scritch!

Scratch!

Crunch!

Piglet sat straight up in bed. Something, outside in the dark, was making **Fierce Sounds**.

"If only Pooh were here," whispered Piglet to himself. "He'd know what to do."

Crackle!

Hiss!

Pop!

Winnie-the-Pooh bounded out of bed and hid behind his chair. Something, outside in the dark, was after his honey!

"If only Piglet were here," mumbled Pooh to himself. "It's so much more friendly with two."

Rabbit and Eeyore had heard the noises, too.

"I say, what's that?" wondered Rabbit. "Must make a plan! **Must rush! Must dash!**"

"Never mind me," grumbled Eeyore. "What's a little noise to one who has the wind whistling through his house all night long? Noise is positively warming to me."

One by one, each of the animals
crept out into the dark to find out
what was making the **strange noises.**
While they were sleeping, snow had
fallen and it took them a moment to
work out where the sound was

coming from. Very cautiously they padded
towards the noises which seemed to
give off an odd light. And there, in a
clearing, was Christopher Robin ...

He had been all around the Forest
gathering up dry sticks and twigs and
he had built up a wonderful bonfire.
It hissed and crackled merrily and lit
the trees with a warm glow, sending
the north wind scampering away.

Christopher Robin invited all his
friends to join him around the
fire - singing songs, telling tales
and roasting marshmallows.

When the marshmallows were all gone they stayed for a long time just staring into the flames.

"Sometimes, waiting for things can be better than the thing you are waiting for," said Piglet, sleepily, to nobody in particular.

"What are you waiting for, Piglet?" asked Pooh anxiously, hoping he wasn't late for something.

"The spring," sighed Piglet happily, as the fire lit up his little pink nose.

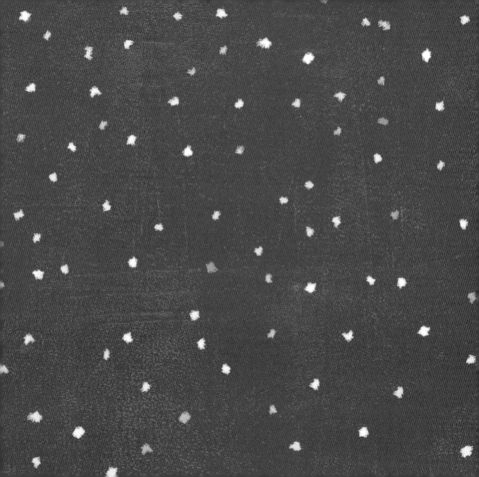

Give the gift of a personalised book

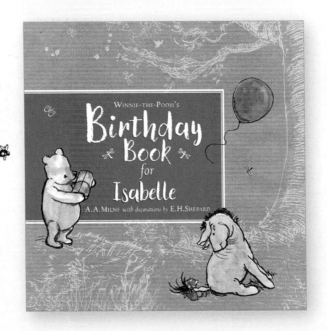

For our full range of books, perfect for every occasion,
visit **shop.egmont.co.uk**

www.egmont.co.uk